By Ari Hill

A GOLDEN BOOK • NEW YORK
Western Publishing Company, Inc., Racine, Wisconsin 53404

 Library of Congress Catalog Card Number: 86-72386 ISBN: 0-307-02165-3
A B C D E F G H I J K L M

The Cabbage Patch Kids were holding a meeting. It was two days before Xavier's birthday, and they wanted to do something really special to help him celebrate it.

"We don't have any money," said Tyler Bo, "so we can't buy him any presents."

"Maybe I could paint him a picture," suggested Rachel Marie.

"That's a good idea," said Otis Lee. "But what can the rest of us do?"

"I have an idea," said Sybil Sadie. "Do you remember Xavier telling us about a show he once saw?"

Some of the 'Kids nodded, and she continued. "It was called a talent show. That's where folks get onstage and sing and dance and sometimes do silly things.

"Well, why don't *we* have a talent show? And since it's my idea, I'll be the director."

Everybody liked Sybil Sadie's idea about the talent show. But they weren't so sure about her running it.

"You know how bossy she can get," said Tyler Bo.

"Yes," said Rebecca Ruby, "but it *is* her idea, and you have to admit that she's a born director."

All of the 'Kids went off on their own to come up with ideas for their acts. They wanted this to be Xavier's best birthday party ever.

Next morning they got together again.

"Well," said Sybil Sadie, "have you all decided what you're doing in the show?"

Everyone nodded.

"OK, then," said Sybil Sadie. "Time for auditions."

"Auditions?" everyone said with surprise.

"Yes," said Sybil Sadie. "You all have to do your acts for me so I can see if they're any good. And you can start, Otis Lee."

"Well, all right," said Otis Lee. "I'm going to tell the story of my greatest adventure. Do you remember the time..."

A few minutes later Otis Lee was still talking, and the other 'Kids were listening closely.

Suddenly Sybil Sadie yawned loudly and said, "I'm almost asleep. Otis Lee, you'd better think up a better—or shorter—adventure story to tell if you want Xavier to stay awake.

"OK, who's next? How about you, Dawson Glen?"

"I'm going to do fancy rope tricks," said Dawson Glen with a grin. And he began to twirl his rope in a big circle.

"There's nothing fancy about a circle," said Sybil Sadie. "And besides, you always do rope tricks. How about doing some other kind of tricks?"

The grin faded from Dawson Glen's face.

"What about you, Marilyn Suzanne?" said Sybil Sadie.

"I was going to do a baton act," said Marilyn Suzanne. "But then I got to thinking I might mess up my clothes. So I'm going to recite a poem instead. Here it is:

"I am a little snowflake,
Up in a cloud so high.
I float down through
the cold, cold air
Till on the earth I lie."

"Hmm," said Sybil Sadie. "You say the words well enough. But I don't think much of that poem. Find something else to recite. Otherwise, you'll just have to twirl the baton after all."

"B-but—" stammered Marilyn Suzanne.

"Next," said Sybil Sadie.

By this time the Cabbage Patch Kids were getting downright upset at the way Sybil Sadie was acting. But Rebecca Ruby told them she thought it was just because Sybil Sadie wanted the best show ever for Xavier. So no one said anything to her.

Then Tyler Bo brought out a bunch of glass tubes filled with different-colored liquids. "I'm going to demonstrate some chemical reactions," he said. He poured a red liquid into a blue one, and it turned white. He poured a green liquid into a yellow one, and it turned black.

When he was finished, he took a little bow, and everyone clapped—except Sybil Sadie.

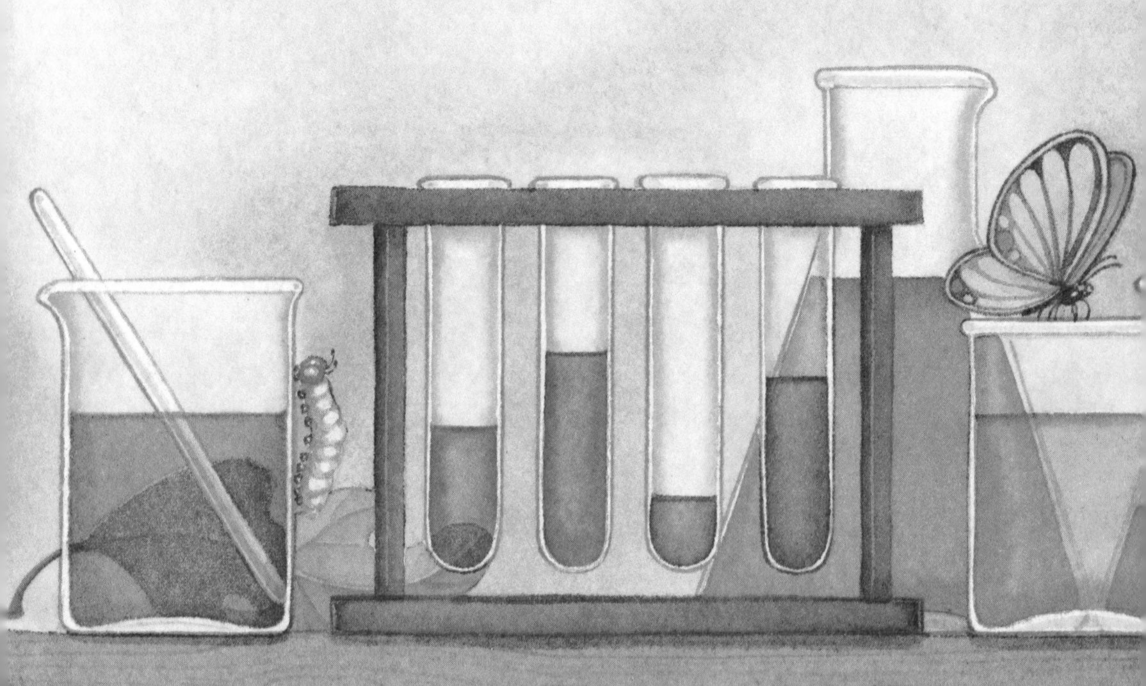

"That was very nice," she said. "Now, what are you going to do in the show?"

"That was it," mumbled Tyler Bo.

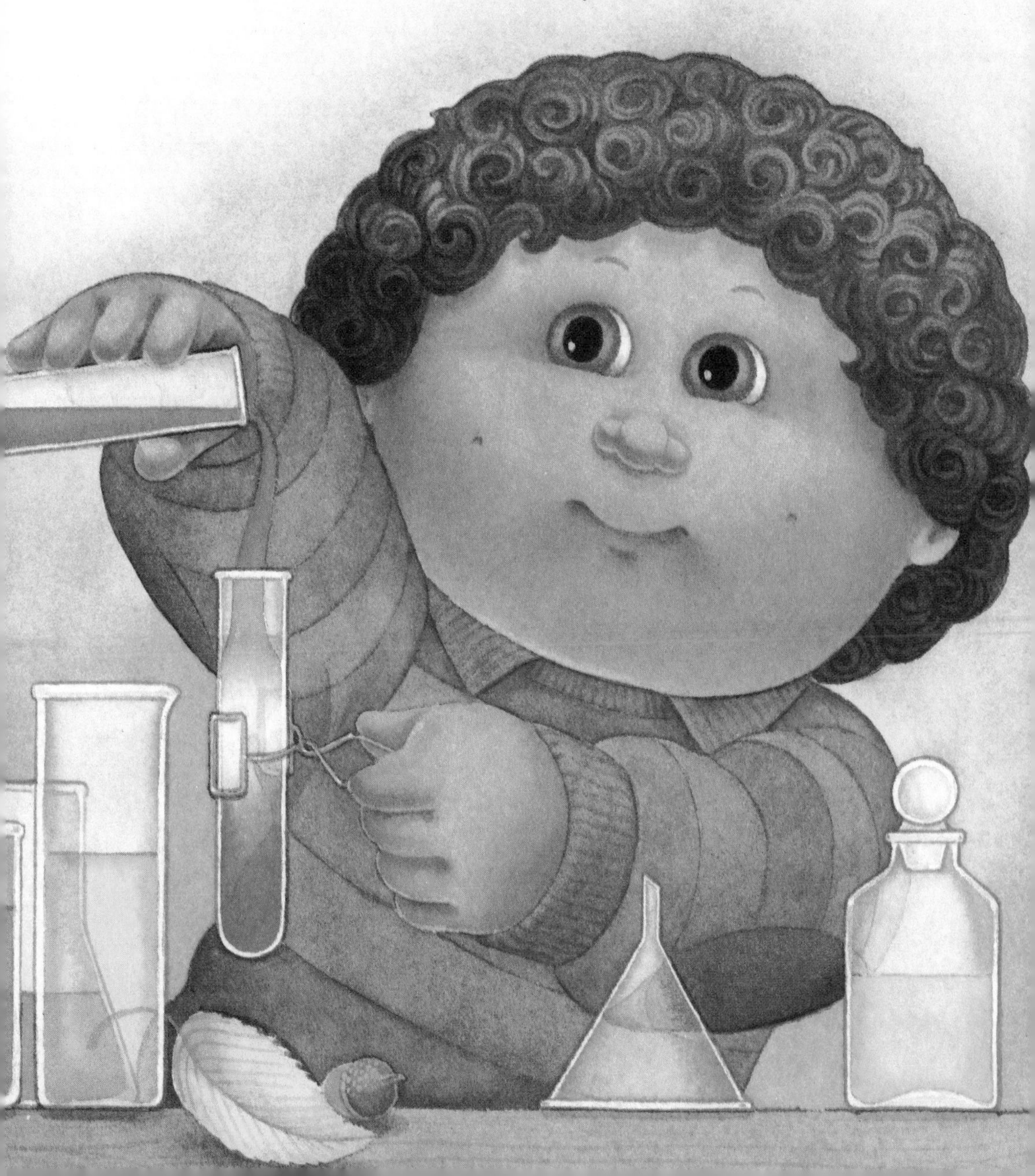

By this time, even Rebecca Ruby had had enough of Sybil Sadie's opinions. And everybody began to tell Sybil Sadie just what they thought of the way she was acting.

It became so noisy in the Patch that no one noticed Colonel Casey landing nearby.

"Harrumph!" he finally said in a loud voice. "Can you all stop your feuding long enough to hear something important? Xavier is on his way here right now!"

"Xavier!" everyone shouted.

Just then, Xavier arrived. "Now, what was all that noise I heard as I was coming toward the Patch?" he asked, smiling.

The 'Kids didn't know what to say. Instead, they all looked down at their feet.

"Don't everybody talk at once," said Xavier.

"Well," Otis Lee started, then stopped.
"Well," said Sybil Sadie, but then she stopped also.

Rebecca Ruby's eyes were full of tears. "Xavier," she said with a sniffle, "we wanted to do something special for your birthday. Sybil Sadie suggested we have a talent show, like the one you told us about. And, well...she was running it the way she thought she should. But when she tried to improve our acts, she made us all mad and hurt our feelings."

Xavier smiled with understanding. "What a wonderful idea for a birthday present," he said.

Turning to Sybil Sadie, he said, "Thanks for trying to make the show super-special. But don't try to make it perfect. I'm sure I'll like every act just the way it is."

The next day was Xavier's birthday. Everyone was feeling a lot better about the show. But in case anybody wasn't, it began with Georgia Ann and Will Henry telling jokes.

Georgia Ann started. "Say, farmer, why did your chicken cross the road?"

And Will Henry answered, "To get to the other side, of course."

Georgia Ann said, "Then why did your duck go across, too?"

And Will Henry answered, "To prove she wasn't chicken, I guess."

All the 'Kids laughed, even Sybil Sadie. But Xavier laughed the loudest of all.

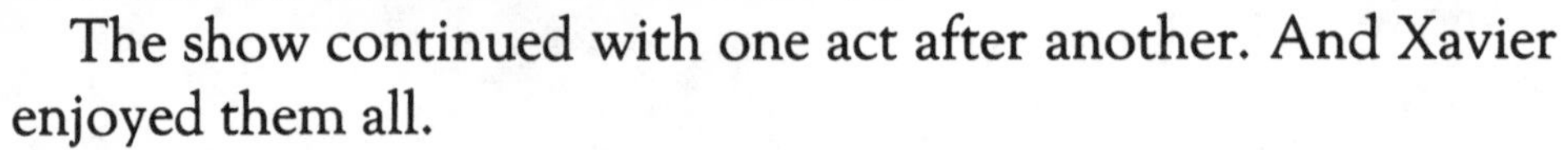

The show continued with one act after another. And Xavier enjoyed them all.

The big finale was a song by Rachel Marie and Rebecca Ruby called "Hum a Little Hum." It started,

"When things look sort of glum,
Just hum a little hum..."

Baby Dodd shook a tambourine almost in rhythm. And just at the right moment, a swarm of BunnyBees flew into the Cabbage Patch and buzzed softly in the background.

When the show was over, Xavier said to Sybil Sadie, "Thank you for the wonderful present."

Then the Cabbage Patch Kids led him to the biggest watermelon-shaped cake he'd ever seen!

Xavier said, "Now, whoever made *this* sure has a lot of talent.... And before I forget, I want to thank you all for the best birthday ever."